ISBN 978-1-332-41427-7
PIBN 10424103

1 MONTH OF
FREE
READING

at

www.ForgottenBooks.com

By purchasing this book you are eligible for one month membership to ForgottenBooks.com, giving you unlimited access to our entire collection of over 700,000 titles via our web site and mobile apps.

To claim your free month visit:

www.forgottenbooks.com/free424103

English
Français
Deutsche
Italiano
Español
Português

www.forgottenbooks.com

Mythology Photography **Fiction**
Fishing Christianity **Art** Cooking
Essays Buddhism Freemasonry
Medicine **Biology** Music **Ancient**
Egypt Evolution Carpentry Physics
Dance Geology **Mathematics** Fitness
Shakespeare **Folklore** Yoga Marketing
Confidence Immortality Biographies
Poetry **Psychology** Witchcraft
Electronics Chemistry History **Law**
Accounting **Philosophy** Anthropology
Alchemy Drama Quantum Mechanics
Atheism Sexual Health **Ancient History**
Entrepreneurship Languages Sport
Paleontology Needlework Islam
Metaphysics Investment Archaeology
Parenting Statistics Criminology
Motivational

"BUBBIE"

BEING·RHYMES
BY *****
A·PROUD·PARENT

PRIVATELY·PRINTED···CHICAGO
MCMXIII *****

THE RALPH FLETCHER SEYMOUR COMPANY
CHICAGO

BUBBIE

BEING RHYMES

BY . . . .

A PROUD PARENT

CONTENTS

FOREWARNING

The first half of the following rhymes was presented in printed form to a few friends in December, 1912. They were taken bodily from Bubbie's record book or kid log and portray with some degree of accuracy events, adventures and crises of the first year of his career. And now another eventful year has passed and been duly entered in the log. This record constitutes the last half of the present volume.

F. M. L.

BUBBIE
BEING RHYMES
BY . . . . .
A PROUD PARENT

DAD'S EXCUSE

I SHOULD have written you before,
　　But all my plans seem bound to balk;
I've thought of you, so don't get sore—
　　I'm busy talking baby-talk.

You want to know about the boy:
　He makes his daddy walk the chalk;
He sure's the source of lots of joy—
　　He's got us talking baby-talk.

His mamma's feeling mighty fine;
　　She wheels him up and down the walk
To give her son a chance to shine—
　　She's always talking baby-talk.

His grandpa and his grandmammas
　　His many charms do loudly hawk;
They're proud as they can be because
　　They too are talking baby-talk.

His uncles both when he arrived,
　　It gave them such an awful shock—
The bashful batches.　They survived
　　To join in talking baby-talk.

Our friends and neighbors everyone—
　　But hark! I think I hear a squawk!
Correct! Good-bye, I've got to run
　　When he himself talks baby-talk!

BUBBIE

MUCH OBLIGED

MY BOY'S requested me to state,
As plain as one so young is able,
The eating irons you sent are great;
And that they are is sure no fable.
As yet—this is in confidence—
He's hardly ready to commence
To wield his feeding tools at table.

The silver spoon's his special joy.
He seems to think it most delicious.
To him it means more than a toy;
He must regard it quite nutritious.
He always grabs it greedily
And with his two teeth speedily
Attacks it, oh, so vicious!

The fork is fated for the shelf
'Till he's arrived at some discretion;
Just now he might harpoon himself,
And that would be a sad digression.
Accept our best beatitude
For these, and know our gratitude
Is full beyond expression.

EARLY OBSERVATIONS

I 'VE lately come from slumberland,
Just landed in this wonderland,
And say, it's hard to understand.

I hope it's not injurious,
But really I'm so curious
It makes me simply furious.

For instance now, I can't make out
What this dark silence is about—
I guess I'll just let out a shout.

Ah, that's the way to wake them up,
Make dad get up and take me up,
And jiggle, bounce and shake me up.

He holds me right-side up with care,
And handles me like something rare
In fragile glass or China-ware.

This bouncing brings a dizziness
The very height of bliss. I guess
My holler did the business.

While I've a lot to learn of course
Of this world's ways, it might be worse:
Of heaps of joy I am the source;

BUBBIE

Besides my papa's pompous pride;
Admirers worship at my side;
Soft mother arms my blushes hide;

I do not have to work or play,
But lie around and loaf all day
And sleep and yawn and grow away;

I've got a good meal ticket, too.
Should roses such as these bestrew
Your path, you'd holler—wouldn't you?

POP'S ELOQUENCE

SINCE you decline to close your eyes
  Regardless of your daddy's sighs,
  Your daddy has a thing or two
  He feels he ought to say to you.

He doubts if you'll appreciate,
  But thinks 'tis due to you to state,
Since you arrived to rule the roost
  Things are not as they used to used.

Your daddy used to take some pride
  In seeming somewhat dignified;
But who could hold their dignity
  While they held you upon their knee?

They say 'tis so and we surmise
  Your little lungs need exercise
But do you think it wise or right
  To exercise so much at night?

You have a most amazing taste.
  Refined amusements simply waste.
With you to really make a hit
  A fellow's got to throw a fit.

And even that may prove a frost:
  To make you smile at any cost
Your grandpa cut such funny jinks,
  And all you did was blink some blinks.

BUBBIE

When mamma's friends come to your bed
  And say, "How cute!" and kiss your head,
Why don't you smile and favor us
  Instead of kicking up a fuss?

You raise a rumpus when you weep—
  Your daddy's talked you fast asleep,
That surely is no compliment,
  But since you are, he too's content.

SLEEP

THOMAS EDISON'S a wonder;
  Always full of new ideas.
  Still I feel impelled to ponder
  Bubbie's 'bout as bright as he is.

Thomas Edison's asserting
  Sleep's a wasteful occupation—
Bubbie's needed no converting
  To that startling observation.

Thomas Edison's persuaded
  But the briefest nap is ample;
Bubbie's got that fairly faded;
  Daddy hardly gets a sample.

Thomas also puts to practice,
  Proving his conclusions proper.
Bubbie—sad but true the fact is—
  Practices upon his popper.

Thomas Edison's a wonder;
  Sleepless nights with ease he weathers.
Still I would not steal his thunder—
  Simply lead me to the feathers.

OH, YOU LUNCH!

I LIKE my little rubber rings;
I like the songs my uncle sings;
I'm fond of such a lot of things—
    But oh, you lunch!

I think my rattle is all right
For it affords me such delight.
I'd like to play with it all night—
    But oh, you lunch!

My bath is lots of fun for me;
I kick and splash and squeal with glee;
I'm most as happy as can be—
    But oh, you lunch!

I have two fascinating feet.
My tender toes are such a treat—
But when it comes to things to eat:
    Oh! you lunch.

EARLY TRAINING

FROM seven until nine o'clock
    You made your popper sing and
      rock,
    And not a snooze could he induce
  So he decided, what's the use;
'Twas time, he said, despite your shouts
  To put you through a course of sprouts.
He took your little squirming hunk
  And popped you in your bunk kerplunk;
And, though you raised an awful roar,
  He gloomed the glim and shut the door.

Your mummie sided with your pop
  To let you cry it out and stop.
To cry it out they found you fit,
  But when it came to stopping, nit.
You whooped it up with all your might
  As though you'd keep it up all night.
They closed the windows not to shock
  Their friends and neighbors in the block;
And settled down to read and sew
  And let you hoe alone your row;

But soon you put their nerves to proof
  The way you fairly raised the roof.
In fact you made so much of it
  They couldn't read and sew a bit—
And after all you were so young—
  Perhaps you might unhinge a lung—

17

BUBBIE

No doubt you really had a pain—
  That something troubled you was plain—
Then panic struck they fairly flew
  To see what they could do for you.
They snatched you up to soothe your brow,
  But all they got from you was "Wow!"
You surely felt abused for fair;
  Your indignation pierced the air;
You scorned their offerings of peace—
  It seemed as though you'd never cease.
When you had fully had your say
  It wasn't quite the break of day.

Pop's not so keen as he was once
About these early training stunts.

OUCH! OR THE FIRST TOOTH

NO WONDER you seemed bound to
gnaw
On each and everything you saw.
They said, who know the ways of
youth,
"Your boy's begun to cut a tooth."
But how could that so much annoy?
It was the tooth that cut my boy.
And now I know that this was true
For yesterday it cut you through.
No wonder you would chew your toes
And try to masticate your clothes;
Most any feller thusly hurt
Would feel inspired to eat his shirt.

NEW MITTS

I'VE got some new mitts,
 And they just give me fits—
 The gink who devised them's a rummy.
 They're built like a bag,
So I've nothing to wag
As there's no place at all for my thummie.

SPLASH! OR THE BATH

THE water gurgles in the tub
   When I go in to have a bath,
     As though it said, "Good morning
     Bub";
And every time it makes me laugh.
Of all the happy sounds I note
   That gladsome gurgle gets my goat.

The water is so soft and warm;
   It always seems to welcome me;
And anchored to my mamma's arm
   I'm not afraid to put to sea.
The water splashes with delight
   And I splash back with all my might.

And when again I'm safe ashore;
   And rubbed and rubbed until I'm dry;
And when I'm powdered aft and fore
   I hear the water laugh "Good-bye."
"Good-bye" it gurgled as it ran;
   I gurgled back "Good-bye old man!"

BEEF-JUICE

WHEN mamma buttons on my bib
It makes me glad in every rib,
For then I know that purty soon
I'll get some beef-juice in a spoon.

She brings it in a little cup,
And when I see her I sit up
And open up my face some wide,
Because the beef-juice goes inside.

So bully does the beef-juice taste
I feel it justifies my haste.
What if it smears me up a bit—
I'd like to dive and roll in it.

And when my brief debauch is o'er
I throw the spoon down on the floor,
And crow and cuckoo like the deuce
To show I'm strong for good beef-juice.

BED-TIME

WHEN darkness comes and all is still
'Tis then the blinky lights are lit;
And though I'm yawning fit to kill
I would not go to bed a bit.

I'm willing to be wiggled free
Of clothes and tickled on my tummy;
And have my nighty hung on me—
But being put in bed is rummy.

My night-cap meal I'm glad to greet
Because I'm famished 'til I'm fed;
But when I've finished, though replete,
I do not wanta be in bed.

I'm left alone without a light—
Take it from me, there's trouble brewing.
I'll not submit to such a plight—
I wanta be where something's doing.

They seem to think the sleeping's fine
When everything is dark and quiet.
Perhaps it is, but as for mine,
That's just the time to raise a riot.

A BIRD OF A BIRD

ONCE when I sat where I could see
The sparrows playing in a tree,
A little sparrow cocked his head
And looked right in at me and said,
"My stars! You're such a tiny tottle
I think it's time you had your bottle."
As I agreed with what I heard
I thought that birdie was a bird.

FIRST WORD

IT CANNOT be you haven't heard
That Bub's connected with a word?
You knew of course that he could screech–
But now he knows a word of speech.

His first attempts at it were wrong;
And then he said it all day long.
Though on his tongue he loves to weigh it,
It doesn't take him long to say it.

The word? 'Tis that that pleases me:
The word is "dog" without the "g."
His popper thinks he's some precocious
Because he says it so ferocious.

At first he had us wondering;
His name was dog for everything.
At last his brain advanced a cog
And now he knows that dog is dog.

EARS

A MATTER of no small concern
  Without a doubt
Is this, so easy to discern:
  My ears stick out.

My mummie looks at me and sighs
  In pensive mood.
I'm wise.   For this her sighs arise:
  My ears protrude.

Pop says they're bully hearing ears,
  That when he's nappin'
I'm always hearing things, he swears,
  That never happen.

My ears may mar the scenery some—
  But why the flurry—
And put my beauty on the bum—
  But I should worry.

NOCTURNE

A
T THREE A. M. I feel possessed
To seek repose on popper's chest;
And, wailing clear in his left ear,
I kick him where he wears his vest.

He buzzes at me like a bee—
A bee about to light on me—
I'll lose a lung but not be stung
As long as I can wiggle free.

And then pop wrestles me around
And sings so loud my song is drowned;
And when I pause to learn the cause
I suddenly am sleeping sound.

What magic thus skidoos the gloom,
Supplanting peace for fret and fume?
Ah, what indeed except the need
Of perching on my pop's buzzoom.

CHUMS

ME AND "Sonny" likes to sit
Side by side upon a rug,
With a cracker in each mit,
Each a crumb bemussed mug.

Sonny eats with proper pause;
Mine I gobble down a whizzin'.
This arrangement suits me 'cause
When mine's gone I just take his'n.

WHY AND WHEN?

Why do you do the things tabooed
Instead of doing what you should?
You have your bell and button-hook,
Your rubber dog, a spoon, a book,
Your dolls, your rattles and your rings,
Beside a lot of other things,
And more reserved upon the shelf
With which you might amuse yourself,
Enough in fact if you'd begin it
To keep you going every minute;
And yet you find more entertainment
In chewing pieces of your raiment.
You much prefer to claw your hair
Or gnaw the varnish off your chair.
And then there's nothing you like better
Than picking fuzz off uncle's sweater,
Unless—this makes your mamma wilt—
It's biting yarn knots off your quilt.
She only has to hear you cough
To know another knot is off.

When will you do the things you should
Instead of just the things tabooed.

EARLY ENGLISH

T ICK TOCK," "how do!",
"Bow-wow," "mew-yew,"
"Doodle doo," "au-to,"
"Ding dong," "no no,"
"Ticks," "tones," "moon-a,"
"Bye, bye," "spoon-a,"
"Tiggle tiggle," "I know,"
"Dog," "ball," "bing!" "oh!",
"Quack, quack," "book," "shoe,"
"Oof, oof," "peek-boo,"
"Ba ba," "moo-moo,"
"Here 'tis," "oo-hoo!";

Many more you command

Which you best understand.

SAND

WHEN I first sat in the sand
The sensation was so blissful
That I laughed to best the band—
Then I tried to eat a fistful.

Eating sand is no great treat.
This conclusion I found fitting:
Maybe sand's not made to eat—
Thought I'd never finish spitting.

FEET-STEPS

TIME was when you supposed your feet
Were good for nothing but to eat,
And then the thought began to dawn,
They might be good to walk upon.

So hanging onto daddy's hand
You took a most unsteady stand,
And, heaving forth two hearty grunts,
You stepped with both your feet at once.

Before you'd fully caught the hang
The floor had biffed you many a bang—
But every feller once begins
Upon a wobbly set of pins.

It really seemed ere you'd begun
To learn to walk you'd learned to run;
And now no music's quite so sweet
As just the patter of those feet.

CPSIA information can be obtained
at www.ICGtesting.com
Printed in the USA
BVHW091356090119
537418BV00031B/1960/P